Precious Princess

Ballerina Necklace
The Birthday Present

Rebecca Parkinson

CWR

Ballerina Necklace

Grandad always said that Daisy was his pretty, precious princess. That's why he gave her a special present.

'Daisy,' he said, 'precious princesses should learn precious secrets. This book will teach you many of the things you need to know as you grow up in this world. Read it well.'

It was then that the adventures began …

It was a beautiful day and Daisy was desperate to go outside to play in the sunshine. She finished her breakfast quickly and danced towards the door.

'Don't forget Polly's coming round in a few minutes,' called Mum, as she gently rocked baby Jack to sleep in the pram.

All of Daisy's good feelings rolled away.

'Oh, Mum,' she grumbled. 'Does she have to? You know I don't like Polly. No one likes her.'

Mum frowned. 'You may not like her Daisy but you can still make an effort to play with her,' she said firmly.

Daisy stomped into the garden and sat down on the swing. She didn't want to play with Polly. Polly always spoilt games and the last time she had come round to play, Daisy's favourite ballerina necklace had disappeared. Daisy was sure Polly had stolen it.

Daisy was still sulking ten minutes later when Mum led Polly into the garden. 'Daisy,' she called. 'Polly's here. I'm sure she'd love a turn on the swing.'

'But *I'm* on it,' answered Daisy rudely. 'She can have a go when I've finished.'

'Daisy!' said Mum firmly. 'Polly is your guest and she would like a go!'

Daisy climbed slowly off the swing and pulled a face at Polly.

'You have a go then,' she snapped. 'I'm going to my room to look for my missing necklace. It disappeared last time *you* were here!'

Polly looked embarrassed and Mum looked furious.

'Daisy!' ordered Mum. 'You can stay in your room until you decide to be nice to Polly. Come on, Polly, we'll go and do some baking.'

Daisy glanced round her room and saw Grandad's special book lying on the bedside table. Grandad always said it would help her as she grew up. She needed some help now! Slowly she opened the book and started to read …

Suddenly the room began to spin. Daisy felt tingles running through her body. She could hear gentle music. She shut her eyes tight. This had happened before … where would she end up this time?

Daisy opened her eyes and found she was standing on a wall near a huge crowd of people. She was wearing a long dress that reached to her ankles and she had sandals on her feet. The sun was shining brightly. All the crowds were peering in the same direction and talking in excited voices. Daisy stretched her neck and carefully stood on tiptoe so that she could see over the head of a small boy who was sitting on his dad's shoulders.

Daisy spotted a group of men walking slowly along the road. They were still a long way off but they seemed to be heading in her direction. The little boy had noticed the same thing.

'They're coming, Dad!' he said in an excited whisper. 'That man at the front … is it Jesus?'

His dad nodded and everyone craned their necks to get a better view.

Suddenly Daisy heard a noise behind her. She glanced round and saw a small man jump onto the wall and disappear into the branches of a nearby sycamore tree. One minute he was there, the next he had gone. No one else seemed to have noticed and for a moment Daisy wondered if she had imagined seeing the man. The noise of the crowd quickly turned her attention back to the road. Jesus and His friends were heading straight towards her!

The crowd grew silent as Jesus came closer. To Daisy's surprise He stopped beside the sycamore tree. Slowly Jesus lifted His head and looked up into the branches.

'Zacchaeus!' He called loudly. 'Come down immediately.'

The people in the crowd glanced at one another, puzzled.

'Why is He talking to a tree?' the little boy whispered to his dad.

A few people sniggered at the boy's comment but Daisy didn't laugh; she knew who Jesus was talking to.

Suddenly the branches of the tree parted and a man's face appeared. The crowd gasped. Jesus looked straight at the man and spoke again.

'Zacchaeus, I must stay at your house today.'

Without hesitation, Zacchaeus jumped out of the tree and began to lead Jesus to his home.

Daisy followed at a distance. She could hear the crowds talking and it was obvious Zacchaeus wasn't a popular man.

'How can Jesus go to Zacchaeus' house?' questioned one man. 'Everyone knows that Zacchaeus is a thief who steals money from us.'

'I know,' answered another lady. 'Jesus can't be that special if He wants to spend time with someone like him!'

The people were still complaining hours later when the door of the house opened and Zacchaeus reappeared. He looked round at the waiting crowd and began to speak.

'I know I have been wrong,' he announced. 'Here and now I will give half of what I own to the poor, and those people that I have stolen from I will pay back four times as much as I have taken.'

As Daisy watched, Jesus came and stood next to Zacchaeus. He gazed round at the crowd with a look in His eyes that made Daisy feel slightly sad.

'Today Zacchaeus has been rescued from a bad life,' said Jesus. 'I have come to help people just like him.'

Some people in the crowd began to grumble but suddenly Daisy understood …

Daisy felt tingles running through her body. She could hear gentle music again and things began to spin. She shut her eyes tight …

When Daisy opened her eyes she was sitting back on her bed with Grandad's book resting on her knee. She smiled. Suddenly it was all clear. She may not like Polly, she might even be fairly sure that she was a thief, but she needed to do exactly what Jesus had done for Zacchaeus. She needed to care about her and be her friend!

Daisy ran downstairs and into the kitchen. Mum and Polly had just finished making cakes and seemed surprised to see her. Daisy marched straight up to Polly.

'I'm sorry,' she said boldly. 'I shouldn't have been rude. Do you want to come and play in my room?'

Polly looked shocked but she nodded and followed Daisy back upstairs.

Once in her bedroom Daisy tried her best to get Polly to play. She showed her the doll's house she had been given for Christmas and the dressing-up box with all the exciting costumes. Polly didn't seem interested in anything. Daisy was about to give up trying when suddenly Polly pulled something out of her pocket. It was Daisy's lost ballerina necklace.

Daisy gasped. So she was right. Polly had stolen it! Daisy had never felt so angry. She opened her mouth to tell Polly what she thought of her but Polly spoke first.

'I'm sorry, Daisy,' she said quietly. 'I did steal it but I felt bad straight away. I didn't know what to do so I brought it with me today. I was going to hide it somewhere and pretend to find it … but then I thought I should own up.'

Daisy looked at Polly who was gazing down at the floor. Part of her wanted to shout, 'I knew you stole it', but she couldn't get the look she had seen on Jesus' face out of her mind. She knew she needed to forgive Polly just like He had forgiven Zacchaeus.

Daisy stepped forward and took hold of Polly's hands. 'We have both done things wrong today,' she said. 'Let's forget about them and just be friends.'

Polly looked up and smiled. 'Thank you,' she whispered.

Suddenly Daisy felt all tingly inside. This time it wasn't the start of an adventure with Grandad's book, just a feeling deep down that she had done the right thing.

'Come on,' she smiled. 'I'll race you to the swing.'

Why not read this story in your own Bible? You will find it in Bible book Luke, chapter 19 verses 1 to 10.

The Birthday Present

Grandad always said that Daisy was his pretty, precious princess. That's why he gave her a special present.

'Daisy,' he said, 'precious princesses should learn precious secrets. This book will teach you many of the things you need to know as you grow up in this world. Read it well.'

It was then that the adventures began …

Daisy lay down on the freshly mown grass and gazed up at the clear blue sky. Birds twittered noisily in the trees and the smell of beautiful flowers filled the air. She lifted the buttercups clasped firmly in her hand and watched as the sunlight danced off their petals. She was glad she had asked Dad to leave a small part of the lawn un-mown for the past few weeks. The small plot had become a mass of yellow and now she had plenty of flowers to carry out her plan.

Daisy sprang up, skipped inside and ran up to her bedroom. Carefully she arranged the buttercups in the small vase on the table beside her bed and stood back to admire them. She had spent hours making the vase, moulding it out of papier maché, covering it with varnish to make it waterproof and painting it in Grandma's favourite colours. The buttercups added the final touch and Daisy smiled happily. She was certain her grandma would be pleased with the present.

'Daisy,' Mum's voice echoed up the stairs. 'Can you get yourself ready and then come down to help. Everyone will be arriving in about half an hour.'

'Of course I can,' Daisy shouted back enthusiastically, a thrill of excitement running through her body. She had been waiting for this day to arrive for weeks!

Today was Grandma's 70th birthday and a surprise party was being held at Daisy's house. The whole week had been spent getting ready, cleaning the house, decorating every room with 'Happy 70th Birthday' banners and making food. Now the moment had almost arrived!

Daisy quickly changed into her party dress and paused to gaze at herself in the long mirror. She swayed gently from side to side, watching the silky material float softly around her legs. Then she twirled round as fast as she could, making the skirt spread out like a ballerina's tutu.

Daisy danced happily down the stairs and into the kitchen. Mum glanced up from where she was piling the last strawberry onto a huge pavlova.

'You look lovely …' she began, but she stopped when she saw the look on Daisy's face.

'What are those?' asked Daisy quietly, pointing to a large pile of presents, in front of which was the biggest arrangement of flowers Daisy had ever seen.

'The presents are from some of the neighbours who knew Grandma when she lived in this house,' Mum explained. 'And the flowers are from the charity shop where Grandma works. It's really kind of them. Grandma will be so pleased.'

Suddenly Daisy's happy world seemed to tumble down. Sadly she wandered back to her room and sat down on the edge of her bed.

After a few minutes Mum joined her.

'What's the matter, Daisy?' she asked.

Daisy pointed at her own little vase of flowers.

'Mine looks rubbish,' she said, trying hard not to cry, 'compared to the ones downstairs.'

The ringing of the doorbell broke the silence.

'I'm sorry, love,' said Mum, sounding flustered. 'But I'll have to go and let the visitors in.'

She bent down to pick up a book from the floor and flicked through the pages.

'This might help you,' said Mum gently, handing the open book to Daisy. 'I'll see you downstairs in a few minutes.'

Daisy looked down at the book in her hands. A tear ran down her cheek and dripped onto the pages. Grandad always said this book would help her as she grew up. She needed some help now! She started to read …

Suddenly the room began to spin. Daisy felt tingles running through her body. She could hear gentle music. She shut her eyes tight. This had happened before … where would she end up this time?

When she opened her eyes Daisy was standing behind a large stone pillar in what appeared to be a long, dimly lit corridor. She was wearing a long dress that reached to her ankles and she had sandals on her feet. Slowly Daisy leaned to one side and peeped out from behind the pillar.

To her surprise, Daisy found herself looking into a large courtyard. In one direction there was a huge flight of stairs leading to one of the most beautiful buildings she had ever seen. Even through half-closed eyes the view still dazzled Daisy, as the sunlight reflected off the golden decoration and marble columns.

Looking in the opposite direction Daisy could see an entrance to the courtyard. She watched as a little boy, holding firmly onto his mum's hand, moved through the gateway and headed towards her.

'I love coming here to the Temple,' the little boy whispered to his mum as they walked past. 'It makes me feel all happy inside and, you never know, we might see Jesus!'

Daisy saw his mum nod towards a man resting against a pillar close by.

'Is that Him?' asked the little boy, wonder shining in his eyes.

His mum smiled and nodded again.

'Yes,' she said quietly. 'But we won't disturb Him. Maybe He just wants some time to Himself.'

Suddenly a loud clatter made Daisy jump. She turned to see an old man emptying a bulging bag full of money into a large box. Daisy was sure he could have emptied the bag more quietly!

As she watched, Daisy saw lots of people repeating the man's action. Each person seemed to make as much noise as they could, as if hoping that everybody would see what large amounts of money they were giving to the Temple.

It was then that Daisy realised that Jesus wasn't taking any notice of these people, despite the loud clattering of their coins. Instead His eyes were following an elderly woman as she slowly made her way towards the collection boxes. Daisy watched her too. She looked different to many of the other people in the courtyard. Her clothes were old and worn and she wasn't carrying a money bag.

As the woman moved nearer, she slowly lifted one hand and slipped two tiny copper coins noiselessly into one of the boxes. Then she turned quietly and walked away.

Daisy could see some people glancing at the woman unkindly, as if they thought her gift was worth nothing. But Daisy could also see Jesus' face. It was almost glowing with happiness, as if He had just seen something beautiful.

Daisy watched as Jesus beckoned to some of His friends.

'Did you see that woman?' Jesus asked them. 'She gave more to God than everybody else. All these other people are rich and gave a tiny bit of the money they have. But that woman is very poor and, out of love for God, she gave everything she had.'

Suddenly Daisy felt tingles running through her body. She could hear gentle music again and things began to spin. She shut her eyes tight …

When Daisy opened her eyes she was sitting back on her bed with Grandad's book still resting on her knee. She smiled. All of a sudden, it was clear. What was important wasn't how big a gift was or how much money it had cost to buy. What really mattered was the love that was behind the gift.

Daisy picked up the little vase of buttercups. Suddenly the size of her present didn't seem to matter any more. She had tried to do something special and Grandma would understand that.

Mum's head popped round the bedroom door.

'You feeling better now?' she asked gently.

Daisy nodded.

'Good,' said Mum, carefully fastening a pink flower clip into Daisy's hair. 'Grandma will be here in five minutes!'

Daisy rushed downstairs to where all her relatives were waiting and placed her buttercups alongside the other presents.

'We're all going to hide in here,' whispered Dad. 'Grandad has rung to say they've set off, so they shouldn't be long.'

Everyone waited in silence. It seemed like ages before the door opened and in walked Grandma.

'Happy birthday!' shouted everyone as they set off their party poppers.

Daisy ran forward and gave Grandma a big hug before leading her towards the pile of presents.

'Are all those for me?' Grandma gasped.

Daisy nodded as Grandma reached out and picked up the vase of buttercups.

'Well, look at these,' she said laughing. 'My favourite flowers in a vase painted with my favourite colours. Someone knew exactly what I would like for my birthday!'

Daisy smiled when she saw the look on Grandma's face. She had seen the same look on someone else's face earlier that day; a look that understood the effort that had gone into giving a special gift. Daisy felt tingly inside. This time it wasn't the start of a new adventure, but the knowledge that she had made Grandma very happy.

Why not read this story in your own Bible? You will find it in Bible book Luke, chapter 21 verses 1 to 4.

Ballerina Necklace + The Birthday Present

For Lydia.
Thank you x

OTHER TITLES IN THIS SERIES INCLUDE:

Precious Princess: Starry Night/On the Beach
Precious Princess: The Picnic/The New Girl
Precious Princess: The Village Fair/The Bridesmaid

Published 2013 by CWR, Waverley Abbey House, Waverley Lane, Farnham, Surrey GU9 8EP, UK. Reprinted 2013. CWR is a Registered Charity – Number 294387 and a Limited Company registered in England – Registration Number 1990308.

Visit www.cwr.org.uk/distributors for a list of National Distributors
Concept development, editing, design and production by CWR
Illustrations by Mike Henson at CWR
Printed and bound in China by C&C Offset Printing Co.,Ltd
ISBN: 978-1-85345-988-7